THE MERCHANTMAN AND THE PIRATE

THE MERCHANTMAN AND THE PIRATE

Charles Reade

North Latitude 23 1/2, Longitude East 113; the time March of this same year; the wind southerly; the port Whampoa in the Canton River. Ships at anchor reared their tall masts, here and there; and the broad stream was enlivened and colored by junks and boats of all sizes and vivid hues, propelled on the screw principle by a great scull at the stern, with projecting handles for the crew to work; and at times a gorgeous mandarin boat, with two great glaring eyes set in the bows, came flying, rowed with forty paddles by an armed crew, whose shields hung on the gunwale and flashed fire in the sunbeams; the mandarin, in conical and buttoned hat, sitting on the top of his cabin calmly smoking Paradise, alias opium, while his gong boomed and his boat flew fourteen miles an hour, and all things scuttled out of his celestial way. And there, looking majestically down on all these water ants, the huge Agra, cynosure of so many loving eyes and loving hearts in England, lay at her moorings; homeward bound.

Her tea not being yet on board, the ship's hull floated high as a castle, and to the subtle, intellectual, doll-faced, bolus-eyed people, that sculled to and fro, busy as bees, though looking forked mushrooms, she sounded like a vast musical shell: for a lusty harmony of many mellow voices vibrated in her great cavities, and made the air ring cheerily around her. The vocalists were the Cyclops, to judge by the tremendous thumps that kept clean time to their sturdy tune. Yet it was but human labor, so heavy and so knowing, that it had called in music to help. It was the third mate and his gang completing his floor to receive the coming tea chests. Yesterday he had stowed his dunnage, many hundred bundles of light flexible canes from Sumatra and Malacca; on these he had laid tons of rough saltpetre, in 200 lb. gunny-bags: and was now mashing it to music, bags and all. His gang of fifteen, naked to the waist, stood in line, with huge wooden beetles, called commanders, and lifted them high and brought them down on the nitre in cadence with true nautical power and unison, singing as follows, with ponderous bump on the last note in each bar:—
Song sung by labor gang.
[Illustration: Song sung by labor gang.]

And so up to fifteen, when the stave was concluded with a shrill "Spell, oh!" and the gang relieved streaming with perspiration. When the saltpetre was well mashed, they rolled ton waterbutts on it, till the floor was like a billiard table. A fleet of chop boats then began to arrive, so many per day, with the tea chests. Mr. Grey proceeded to lay the first tier on his saltpetre floor, and then built the chests, tier upon tier, beginning at the sides, and leaving in the middle a lane somewhat narrower than a tea chest. Then he applied a screw jack to the chests on both sides, and so enlarged his central aperture, and forced the remaining tea chests in; and behold the enormous cargo packed as tight as ever shopkeeper packed a box—19,806 chests, 60 half chests, 50 quarter chests.

While Mr. Grey was contemplating his work with singular satisfaction, a small boat from Canton came alongside, and Mr. Tickell, midshipman, ran up the side, skipped on the quarter-deck, saluted it first, and then the first mate; and gave him a line from the captain, desiring him to take the ship down to Second Bar—for her water—at the turn of the tide.

Two hours after receipt of this order the ship swung to the ebb. Instantly Mr. Sharpe unmoored, and the Agra began her famous voyage, with her head at right angles to her course; for the wind being foul, all Sharpe could do was to set his topsails, driver, and jib, and keep her in the tide way, and clear of the numerous craft, by backing or filling as the case required; which he did with considerable dexterity, making the sails steer the helm for the nonce: he crossed the Bar at sunset, and brought to with the best bower anchor in five fathoms and a half. Here they began to take in their water, and on the fifth day the six-oared gig was ordered up to Canton for the captain. The next afternoon he passed the ship in her, going down the river, to Lin Tin, to board the Chinese admiral for his chop, or permission to leave China. All night the Agra showed three lights at her mizzen peak for him, and kept a sharp lookout. But he did not come: he was having a very serious talk with the Chinese admiral; at daybreak, however, the gig was reported in sight: Sharpe told one of the midshipmen to call the boatswain and man the side. Soon the gig ran alongside; two of the ship's boys jumped like monkeys over the bulwarks, lighting, one on the main channels, the other on the mid-ship port, and put the side ropes assiduously in the captain's hands; he bestowed a slight paternal smile on them, the first the imps had ever received from an officer, and went lightly up the sides. The moment his foot touched the deck, the boatswain gave a frightful shrill whistle; the men at the sides uncovered, the captain saluted the quarter-deck, and all the officers saluted him, which he returned, and stepping for a moment to the weather side of his deck, gave the loud command, "All hands heave anchor." He then directed Mr. Sharpe to get what sail he could on the ship, the wind being now westerly, and dived into his cabin.

The boatswain piped three shrill pipes, and "All hands up anchor" was thrice repeated forward, followed by private admonitions, "Rouse and bitt!"

"Show a leg!" etc., and up tumbled the crew with "homeward bound" written on their tanned faces.

(Pipe.) "Up all hammocks!"

In ten minutes the ninety and odd hammocks were all stowed neatly in the netting, and covered with a snowy hammock cloth; and the hands were active, unbitting the cable, shipping the capstan bars, etc.

"All ready below, sir," cried a voice.

"Man the bars," returned Mr. Sharpe from the quarter-deck. "Play up, fifer. Heave away!"

Out broke the merry fife with a rhythmical tune, and tramp, tramp, tramp went a hundred and twenty feet round and round, and, with brawny chests pressed tight against the capstan bars, sixty fine fellows walked the ship up to her anchor, drowning the fife at intervals with their sturdy song, as pat to their feet as an echo:

Heave with a will ye jolly boys,
    Heave around:
We're off from Chainee, jolly boys,
    Homeward bound.

"Short stay apeak, sir," roars the boatswain from forward.

"Unship the bars. Way aloft. Loose sails. Let fall!"

The ship being now over her anchor, and the topsails set, the capstan bars were shipped again, the men all heaved with a will, the messenger grinned, the anchor was torn out of China with a mighty heave, and then run up with a luff tackle and secured; the ship's head cast to port:

"Up with a jib! man the topsail halyards! all hands make sail!" Round she came slow and majestically; the sails filled, and the good ship bore away for England.

She made the Bogue forts in three or four tacks, and there she had to come to again for another chop, China being a place as hard to get into as Heaven, and to get out of as—Chancery. At three P. M. she was at Macao, and hove to four miles from the land, to take in her passengers.

A gun was fired from the forecastle. No boats came off. Sharpe began to fret: for the wind, though light, had now got to the N.W., and they were wasting it. After a while the captain came on deck, and ordered all the carronades to be scaled. The eight heavy reports bellowed the great ship's impatience across the water, and out pulled two boats with the passengers. While they were coming, Dodd sent and ordered the gunner to load the carronades with shot, and secure and apron them....

The Agra had already shown great sailing qualities: the log was hove at sundown and gave eleven knots; so that with a good breeze abaft few fore-and-aft-rigged pirates could overhaul her. And this wind carried her swiftly past one nest of them at all events; the Ladrone Isles. At nine P. M. all the lights were ordered out. Mrs. Beresford had brought a novel on board, and refused to comply; the master-at-arms insisted; she threatened him with the vengeance of the Company, the premier, and the nobility and gentry of the British realm. The master-at-arms, finding he had no chance in argument, doused the glim—pitiable resource of a weak disputant—then basely fled the rhetorical consequences.

The northerly breeze died out, and light variable winds baffled the ship. It was the 6th April ere she passed the Macclesfield Bank in latitude 16. And now they sailed for many days out of sight of land; Dodd's chest expanded: his main anxiety at this part of the voyage lay in the state cabin; of all the perils of the sea none shakes a sailor like fire. He set a watch day and night on that spoiled child.

On the 1st of May they passed the great Nantuna, and got among the Bornese and Malay Islands: at which the captain's glass began to sweep the horizon again: and night and day at the dizzy foretop-gallant-masthead he perched an eye.

They crossed the line in longitude 107, with a slight breeze, but soon fell into the Dolddrums. A dead calm, and nothing to do but kill time....

After lying a week like a dead log on the calm but heaving waters came a few light puffs in the upper air and inflated the topsails only: the ship crawled southward, the crew whistling for wind.

At last, one afternoon, it began to rain, and after the rain came a gale from the eastward. The watchful skipper saw it purple the water to windward, and ordered the topsails to be reefed and the lee ports closed. This last order seemed an excess of precaution; but Dodd was not yet thoroughly acquainted with his ship's qualities: and the hard cash round his neck made him cautious. The lee ports were closed, all but one, and that was lowered. Mr. Grey was working a problem in his cabin, and wanted a little light and a little air, so he just dropped his port; but, not to deviate from the spirit of his captain's instructions, he fastened a tackle to it; that he might have mechanical force to close it with should the ship lie over.

Down came the gale with a whoo, and made all crack. The ship lay over pretty much, and the sea poured in at Mr. Grey's port. He applied his purchase to close it. But though his tackle gave him the force of a dozen hands, he might as well have tried to move a mountain: on the contrary, the tremendous sea rushed in and burst the port wide open. Grey, after a vain struggle with its might, shrieked for help; down tumbled the nearest hands, and hauled on the tackle in vain. Destruction was rushing on the ship, and on them first. But meantime the captain, with a shrewd guess at the general nature of the danger he could not see, had roared out, "Slack the main sheet!" The ship righted, and the port came flying to, and terror-stricken men breathed hard, up to their waists in water and floating boxes. Grey barred the unlucky port, and went aft, drenched in body, and wrecked in mind, to report his own fault. He found the captain looking grim as death. He told him, almost crying, what he had done, and how he had miscalculated the power of the water.

Dodd looked and saw his distress. "Let it be a lesson sir," said he, sternly. "How many ships have been lost by this in fair weather, and not a man saved to tell how the craft was fooled away?"

"Captain, bid me fling myself over the side, and I'll do it."

"Humph! I'm afraid I can't afford to lose a good officer for a fault he—will—never—repeat."

It blew hard all night and till twelve the next day. The Agra showed her weak point: she rolled abominably. A dirty night came on. At eight bells Mr. Grey touched by Dodd's clemency, and brimful of zeal, reported a light in Mrs. Beresford's cabin. It had been put out as usual by the master-at-arms; but the refractory one had relighted it.

"Go and take it away," said Dodd.

Soon screams were heard from the cabin. "Oh! mercy! mercy! I will not be drowned in the dark."

Dodd, who had kept clear of her so long, went down and tried to reassure her.

"Oh, the tempest! the tempest!" she cried. "AND TO BE DROWNED IN THE DARK!"

"Tempest? It is blowing half a gale of wind; that is all."

"Half a gale! Ah, that is the way you always talk to us ladies. Oh, pray give me my light, and send me a clergyman!"

Dodd took pity, and let her have her light, with a midshipman to watch it. He even made her a hypocritical promise that, should there be one grain of danger, he would lie to; but said he must not make a foul wind of a fair one for a few lurches. The Agra broke plenty of glass and crockery though with her fair wind and her lee lurches.

Wind down at noon next day, and a dead calm.

At two P.M. the weather cleared; the sun came out high in heaven's centre; and a balmy breeze from the west.

At six twenty-five, the grand orb set calm and red, and the sea was gorgeous with miles and miles of great ruby dimples: it was the first glowing smile of southern latitude. The night stole on so soft, so clear, so balmy, all were loth to close their eyes on it: the passengers lingered long on deck, watching the Great Bear dip, and the Southern Cross rise, and overhead a whole heaven of glorious stars most of us have never seen, and never shall see in this world. No belching smoke obscured, no plunging paddles deafened; all was musical; the soft air sighing among the sails; the phosphorescent water bubbling from the ship's bows; the murmurs from little knots of men on deck subdued by the great calm: home seemed near, all danger far; Peace ruled the sea, the sky, the heart: the ship, making a track of white fire on the deep, glided gently yet swiftly homeward, urged by snowy sails piled up like alabaster towers against a violet sky, out of which looked a thousand eyes of holy tranquil fire. So melted the sweet night away.

Now carmine streaks tinged the eastern sky at the water's edge: and that water blushed; now the streaks turned orange, and the waves below them sparkled. Thence splashes of living gold flew and settled on the ship's white sails, the deck, and the faces; and with no more prologue, being so near the line, up came majestically a huge, fiery, golden sun, and set the sea flaming liquid topaz.

Instantly the lookout at the foretop-gallant-masthead hailed the deck below.

"STRANGE SAIL! RIGHT AHEAD!"

The strange sail was reported to Captain Dodd, then dressing in his cabin. He came soon after on deck and hailed the lookout: "Which way is she standing?"

"Can't say, sir. Can't see her move any."

Dodd ordered the boatswain to pipe to breakfast; and taking his deck glass went lightly up to the foretop-gallant-mast-crosstrees. Thence, through the light haze of a glorious morning, he espied a long low schooner, lateen-rigged, lying close under Point Leat, a small island about nine miles distant on the weather bow; and nearly in the Agra's course then approaching the Straits of Gaspar, 4 Latitude S.

"She is hove to," said Dodd, very gravely.

At eight o'clock, the stranger lay about two miles to windward; and still hove to.

By this time all eyes were turned upon her, and half a dozen glasses. Everybody, except the captain, delivered an opinion. She was a Greek lying to for water: she was a Malay coming north with canes, and short of hands: she was a pirate watching the Straits.

The captain leaned silent and sombre with his arms on the bulwarks, and watched the suspected craft.

Mr. Fullalove joined the group, and levelled a powerful glass, of his own construction. His inspection was long and minute, and, while the glass was at his eye, Sharpe asked him half in a whisper, could he make out anything?

"Wal," said he, "the varmint looks considerably snaky." Then, without moving his glass, he let drop a word at a time, as if the facts were trickling into his telescope at the lens, and out at the sight. "One—two—four—seven, false ports."

There was a momentary murmur among the officers all round. But British sailors are undemonstrative: Colonel Kenealy, strolling the deck with a cigar, saw they were watching another ship with maritime curiosity, and making comments; but he discerned no particular emotion nor anxiety in what they said, nor in the grave low tones they said it in. Perhaps a brother seaman would though.

The next observation that trickled out of Fullalove's tube was this: "I judge there are too few hands on deck, and too many—white—eyeballs—glittering at the portholes."

"Confound it!" muttered Bayliss, uneasily; "how can you see that?"

Fullalove replied only by quietly handing his glass to Dodd. The captain, thus appealed to, glued his eye to the tube.

"Well, sir; see the false ports, and the white eyebrows?" asked Sharpe, ironically.

"I see this is the best glass I ever looked through," said Dodd doggedly, without interrupting his inspection.

"I think he is a Malay pirate," said Mr. Grey.

Sharpe took him up very quickly, and, indeed, angrily: "Nonsense! And if he is, he won't venture on a craft of this size."

"Says the whale to the swordfish," suggested Fullalove, with a little guttural laugh.

The captain, with the American glass at his eye, turned half round to the man at the wheel: "Starboard!"

"Starboard it is."

"Steer South South East."

"Ay, ay, sir." And the ship's course was thus altered two points.

This order lowered Dodd fifty per cent in Mr. Sharpe's estimation. He held his tongue as long as he could: but at last his surprise and dissatisfaction burst out of him, "Won't that bring him out on us?"

"Very likely, sir," replied Dodd.

"Begging your pardon, captain, would it not be wiser to keep our course, and show the blackguard we don't fear him?"

"When we do? Sharpe, he has made up his mind an hour ago whether to lie still, or bite; my changing my course two points won't change his mind; but it may make him declare it; and I must know what he does intend, before I run the ship into the narrows ahead."

"Oh, I see," said Sharpe, half convinced.

The alteration in the Agra's course produced no movement on the part of the mysterious schooner. She lay to under the land still, and with only a few hands on deck, while the Agra edged away from her and entered the straits between Long Island and Point Leat, leaving the schooner about two miles and a half distant to the N.W.

Ah! The stranger's deck swarms black with men.

His sham ports fell as if by magic, his guns grinned through the gaps like black teeth; his huge foresail rose and filled, and out he came in chase.

The breeze was a kiss from Heaven, the sky a vaulted sapphire, the sea a million dimples of liquid, lucid, gold....

The way the pirate dropped the mask, showed his black teeth, and bore up in chase, was terrible: so dilates and bounds the sudden tiger on his unwary prey. There were stout hearts among the officers of the peaceful Agra; but danger in a new form shakes the brave; and this was their first pirate: their dismay broke out in ejaculations not loud but deep....

"Sharpe," said Dodd, in a tone that conveyed no suspicion of the newcomer, "set the royals, and flying jib.—Port!"

"Port it is," cried the man at the helm.

"Steer due South!" And, with these words in his mouth, Dodd dived to the gun deck.

By this time elastic Sharpe had recovered the first shock; and the order to crowd sail on the ship galled his pride and his manhood; he muttered, indignantly, "The white feather!" This eased his mind, and he obeyed orders briskly as ever. While he and his hands were setting every rag the ship could carry on that tack, the other officers, having unluckily no orders to execute, stood gloomy and helpless, with their eyes glued, by a sort of sombre fascination, on that coming fate....

Realize the situation, and the strange incongruity between the senses and the mind in these poor fellows! The day had ripened its beauty; beneath a purple heaven shone, sparkled, and laughed a blue sea, in whose waves the tropical sun seemed to have fused his beams; and beneath that fair, sinless, peaceful sky, wafted by a balmy breeze over those smiling, transparent, golden waves, a bloodthirsty Pirate bore down on them with a crew of human tigers; and a lady babble babble babble babble babble babble babbled in their quivering ears.

But now the captain came bustling on deck, eyed the loftier sails, saw they were drawing well, appointed four midshipmen in a staff to convey his orders; gave Bayliss charge of the carronades, Grey of the cutlasses, and directed Mr. Tickell to break the bad news gently to Mrs. Beresford, and to take her below to the orlop deck; ordered the purser to serve out beef, biscuit, and grog to all hands, saying, "Men can't work on an empty stomach: and fighting is hard work;" then beckoned the officers to come round him. "Gentlemen," said he, confidentially, "in crowding sail on this ship I had no hope of escaping that fellow on this tack, but I was, and am, most anxious to gain the open sea, where I can square my yards and run for it, if I see a chance. At present I shall carry on till he comes up within range: and then, to keep the Company's canvas from being shot to rags, I shall shorten sail; and to save ship and cargo and all our lives, I shall fight while a plank of her swims. Better to be killed in hot blood than walk the plank in cold."

The officers cheered faintly: the captain's dogged resolution stirred up theirs....

"Shorten sail to the taupsles and jib, get the colors ready on the halyards, and then send the men aft...."

Sail was no sooner shortened, and the crew ranged, than the captain came briskly on deck, saluted, jumped on a carronade, and stood erect. He was not the man to show the crew his forebodings.

(Pipe.) "Silence fore and aft."

"My men, the schooner coming up on our weather quarter is a Portuguese pirate. His character is known; he scuttles all the ships he boards, dishonors the women, and murders the crew. We cracked on to get out of the narrows, and now we have shortened sail to fight this blackguard, and teach him not to molest a British ship. I promise, in the Company's name, twenty pounds prize money to every man before the mast if we beat him off or out manoeuvre him; thirty if we sink him; and forty if we tow him astern into a friendly port. Eight guns are clear below, three on the weather side, five on the lee; for, if he knows his business, he will come up on the lee quarter: if he doesn't, that is no fault of yours nor mine. The muskets are all loaded, the cutlasses ground like razors—"

"Hurrah!"

"We have got women to defend—"

"Hurrah!"

"A good ship under our feet, the God of justice overhead, British hearts in our bosoms, and British colors flying—run 'em up!—over our heads." (The ship's colors flew up to the fore, and the Union Jack to the mizzen peak.) "Now lads, I mean to fight this ship while a plank of her (stamping on the deck) swims beneath my foot and—WHAT DO YOU SAY?"

The reply was a fierce "hurrah!" from a hundred throats, so loud, so deep, so full of volume, it made the ship vibrate, and rang in the creeping-on pirate's ears. Fierce, but cunning, he saw mischief in those shortened sails, and that Union Jack, the terror of his tribe, rising to a British cheer; he lowered his mainsail, and crawled up on the weather quarter. Arrived within a cable's length, he double reefed his foresail to reduce his rate of sailing nearly to that of the ship; and the next moment a tongue of flame, and then a gash of smoke, issued from his lee bow, and the ball flew screaming like a seagull over the Agra's mizzen top. He then put his helm up, and fired his other bow-chaser, and sent the shot hissing and skipping on the water past the ship. This prologue made the novices wince. Bayliss wanted to reply with a carronade; but Dodd forbade him sternly, saying, "If we keep him aloof we are done for."

The pirate drew nearer, and fired both guns in succession, hulled the Agra amidships, and sent an eighteen pound ball through her foresail. Most of the faces were pale on the quarter-deck; it was very trying to be shot at, and hit, and make no return. The next double discharge sent one shot smash through the stern cabin window, and splintered the bulwark with another, wounding a seaman slightly.

"LIE DOWN FORWARD!" shouted Dodd, through his trumpet. "Bayliss, give him a shot."

The carronade was fired with a tremendous report, but no visible effect. The pirate crept nearer, steering in and out like a snake to avoid the carronades, and firing those two heavy guns alternately into the devoted ship. He hulled the Agra now nearly every shot.

The two available carronades replied noisily, and jumped as usual; they sent one thirty-two pound shot clean through the schooner's deck and side; but that was literally all they did worth speaking of.

"Curse them!" cried Dodd; "load them with grape! They are not to be trusted with ball. And all my eighteen-pounders dumb! The coward won't come alongside and give them a chance."

At the next discharge the pirate chipped the mizzen mast, and knocked a sailor into dead pieces on the forecastle. Dodd put his helm down ere the smoke cleared, and got three carronades to bear, heavily laden with grape. Several pirates fell, dead or wounded, on the crowded deck, and some holes appeared in the foresail; this one interchange was quite in favor of the ship.

But the lesson made the enemy more cautious; he crept nearer, but steered so adroitly, now right astern, now on the quarter, that the ship could seldom bring more than one carronade to bear, while he raked her fore and aft with grape and ball.

In this alarming situation, Dodd kept as many of the men below as possible; but, for all he could do four were killed and seven wounded.

Fullalove's word came too true: it was the swordfish and the whale: it was a fight of hammer and anvil; one hit, the other made a noise. Cautious and cruel, the pirate hung on the poor hulking creature's quarters and raked her at point blank distance. He made her pass a bitter time. And her captain! To see the splintering hull, the parting shrouds, the shivered gear, and hear the shrieks and groans of his wounded; and he unable to reply in kind! The sweat of agony poured down his face. Oh, if he could but reach the open sea, and square his yards, and make a long chase of it; perhaps fall in with aid. Wincing under each heavy blow, he crept doggedly, patiently on, towards that one visible hope.

At last, when the ship was cloven with shot, and peppered with grape, the channel opened: in five minutes more he could put her dead before the wind.

No. The pirate, on whose side luck had been from the first, got half a broadside to bear at long musket shot, killed a midshipman by Dodd's side, cut away two of the Agra's mizzen shrouds, wounded the gaff: and cut the jib stay; down fell the powerful sail into the water, and dragged across the ship's forefoot, stopping her way to the open sea she panted for, the mates groaned; the crew cheered stoutly, as British tars do in any great disaster; the pirates yelled with ferocious triumph, like the devils they looked.

But most human events, even calamities, have two sides. The Agra being brought almost to a standstill, the pirate forged ahead against his will, and the combat took a new and terrible form. The elephant gun popped, and the rifle cracked, in the Agra's mizzen top, and the man at the pirate's helm jumped into the air and fell dead: both Theorists claimed him. Then the three carronades peppered him hotly; and he hurled an iron shower back with fatal effect. Then at last the long 18-pounders on the gun-deck got a word in. The old Niler was not the man to miss a vessel alongside in a quiet sea; he sent two round shot clean through him; the third splintered his bulwark, and swept across his deck.

"His masts! fire at his masts!" roared Dodd to Monk, through his trumpet; he then got the jib clear, and made what sail he could without taking all the hands from the guns.

This kept the vessels nearly alongside a few minutes, and the fight was hot as fire. The pirate now for the first time hoisted his flag. It was black as ink. His crew yelled as it rose: the Britons, instead of quailing, cheered with fierce derision: the pirate's wild crew of yellow Malays, black chinless Papuans, and bronzed Portuguese, served their side guns, 12-pounders, well and with ferocious cries; the white Britons, drunk with battle now, naked to the waist, grimed with powder, and spotted like leopards with blood, their own and their mates', replied with loud undaunted cheers, and deadly hail of grape from the quarterdeck; while the master gunner and his mates loading with a rapidity the mixed races opposed could not rival, hulled the schooner well between wind and water, and then fired chain shot at her masts, as ordered, and began to play the mischief with her shrouds and rigging. Meantime, Fullalove and Kenealy, aided by Vespasian, who loaded, were quietly butchering the pirate crew two a minute, and hoped to settle the question they were fighting for; smooth-bore v. rifle: but unluckily neither fired once without killing; so "there was nothing proven."

The pirate, bold as he was, got sick of fair fighting first; he hoisted his mainsail and drew rapidly ahead, with a slight bearing to windward, and dismounted a carronade and stove in the ship's quarter-boat, by way of a parting kick.

The men hurled a contemptuous cheer after him; they thought they had beaten him off. But Dodd knew better. He was but retiring a little way to make a more deadly attack than ever: he would soon wear, and cross the Agra's defenceless bows, to rake her fore and aft at pistol-shot distance; or grapple, and board the enfeebled ship two hundred strong.

Dodd flew to the helm, and with his own hands put it hard aweather, to give the deck guns one more chance, the last, of sinking or disabling the Destroyer. As the ship obeyed, and a deck gun bellowed below him, he saw a vessel running out from Long Island, and coming swiftly up on his lee quarter.

It was a schooner. Was she coming to his aid?

Horror! A black flag floated from her foremast head.

While Dodd's eyes were staring almost out of his head at this death-blow to hope, Monk fired again; and just then a pale face came close to Dodd's, and a solemn voice whispered in his ear: "Our ammunition is nearly done!"

Dodd seized Sharpe's hand convulsively, and pointed to the pirate's consort coming up to finish them; and said, with the calm of a brave man's despair, "Cutlasses! and die hard!"

At that moment the master gunner fired his last gun. It sent a chain shot on board the retiring pirate, took off a Portuguese head and spun it clean into the sea ever so far to windward, and cut the schooner's foremast so nearly through that it trembled and nodded, and presently snapped with a loud crack, and came down like a broken tree, with the yard and sail; the latter overlapping the deck and burying itself, black flag and all, in the sea; and there, in one moment, lay the Destroyer buffeting and wriggling—like a heron on the water with its long wing broken—an utter cripple.

The victorious crew raised a stunning cheer.

"Silence!" roared Dodd, with his trumpet. "All hands make sail!"

He set his courses, bent a new jib, and stood out to windward close hauled, in hopes to make a good offing, and then put his ship dead before the wind, which was now rising to a stiff breeze. In doing this he crossed the crippled pirate's bows, within eighty yards; and sore was the temptation to rake him; but his ammunition being short, and his danger being imminent from the other pirate, he had the self-command to resist the great temptation.

He hailed the mizzen top: "Can you two hinder them from firing that gun?"

"I rather think we can," said Fullalove, "eh, colonel?" and tapped his long rifle.

The ship no sooner crossed the schooner's bows than a Malay ran forward with a linstock. Pop went the colonel's ready carbine, and the Malay fell over dead, and the linstock flew out of his hand. A tall Portuguese, with a movement of rage, snatched it up, and darted to the gun; the Yankee rifle cracked, but a moment too late. Bang! went the pirate's bow-chaser, and crashed into the Agra's side, and passed nearly through her.

"Ye missed him! Ye missed him!" cried the rival theorist, joyfully. He was mistaken: the smoke cleared, and there was the pirate captain leaning wounded against the mainmast with a Yankee bullet in his shoulder, and his crew uttering yells of dismay and vengeance. They jumped, and raged, and brandished their knives and made horrid gesticulations of revenge; and the white eyeballs of the Malays and Papuans glittered fiendishly; and the wounded captain raised his sound arm and had a signal hoisted to his consort, and she bore up in chase, and jamming her fore lateen flat as a board, lay far nearer the wind than the Agra could, and sailed three feet to her two besides. On this superiority being made clear, the situation of the merchant vessel, though not so utterly desperate as before Monk fired his lucky shot, became pitiable enough. If she ran before the wind, the fresh pirate would cut her off: if she lay to windward, she might postpone the inevitable and fatal collision with a foe as strong as that she had only escaped by a rare piece of luck; but this would give the crippled pirate time to refit and unite to destroy her. Add to this the failing ammunition, and the thinned crew!

Dodd cast his eyes all around the horizon for help.

The sea was blank.

The bright sun was hidden now; drops of rain fell, and the wind was beginning to sing; and the sea to rise a little.

"Gentlemen," said he, "let us kneel down and pray for wisdom, in this sore strait."

He and his officers kneeled on the quarter-deck. When they rose, Dodd stood rapt about a minute; his great thoughtful eye saw no more the enemy, the sea, nor anything external; it was turned inward. His officers looked at him in silence.

"Sharpe," said he, at last, 'there must be a way out of them with such a breeze as this is now; if we could but see it."

"Ay, if," groaned Sharpe.

Dodd mused again.

"About ship!" said he, softly, like an absent man.

"Ay, ay, sir!"

"Steer due north!" said he, still like one whose mind was elsewhere.

While the ship was coming about, he gave minute orders to the mates and the gunner, to ensure co-operation in the delicate and dangerous manoeuvres that were sure to be on hand.

The wind was W.N.W.: he was standing north: one pirate lay on his lee beam stopping a leak between wind and water, and hacking the deck clear of his broken masts and yards. The other fresh, and thirsting for the easy prey, came up to weather on him and hang on his quarter, pirate fashion.

When they were distant about a cable's length, the fresh pirate, to meet the ship's change of tactics, changed his own, luffed up, and gave the ship a broadside, well aimed but not destructive, the guns being loaded with ball.

Dodd, instead of replying immediately, put his helm hard up and ran under the pirate's stern, while he was jammed up in the wind, and with his five eighteen-pounders raked him fore and aft, then paying off, gave him three carronades crammed with grape and canister; the almost simultaneous discharge of eight guns made the ship tremble, and enveloped her in thick smoke; loud shrieks and groans were heard from the schooner; the smoke cleared; the pirate's mainsail hung on deck, his jib-boom was cut off like a carrot and the sail struggling; his foresail looked lace, lanes of dead and wounded lay still or writhing on his deck and his lee scuppers ran blood into the sea. Dodd squared his yards and bore away.

The ship rushed down the wind, leaving the schooner staggered and all abroad. But not for long; the pirate wore and fired his bow chasers at the now flying Agra, split one of the carronades in two, and killed a Lascar, and made a hole in the foresail; this done, he hoisted his mainsail again in a trice, sent his wounded below, flung his dead overboard, to the horror of their foes, and came after the flying ship, yawning and firing his bow chasers. The ship was silent. She had no shot to throw away. Not only did she take these blows like a coward, but all signs of life disappeared on her, except two men at the wheel, and the captain on the main gangway.

Dodd had ordered the crew out of the rigging, armed them with cutlasses, and laid them flat on the forecastle. He also compelled Kenealy and Fullalove to come down out of harm's way, no wiser on the smooth-bore question than they went up.

The great patient ship ran environed by her foes; one destroyer right in her course, another in her wake, following her with yells of vengeance, and pounding away at her—but no reply.

Suddenly the yells of the pirates on both sides ceased, and there was a moment of dead silence on the sea.

Yet nothing fresh had happened.

Yes, this had happened: the pirates to windward, and the pirates to leeward, of the Agra, had found out, at one and the same moment, that the merchant captain they had lashed, and bullied, and tortured, was a patient but tremendous man. It was not only to rake the fresh schooner he had put his ship before the wind, but also by a double, daring, master-stroke to hurl his monster ship bodily on the other. Without a foresail she could never get out of his way. Her crew had stopped the leak, and cut away and unshipped the broken foremast, and were stepping a new one, when they saw the huge ship bearing down in full sail. Nothing easier than to slip out of her way could they get the foresail to draw; but the time was short, the deadly intention manifest, the coming destruction swift. After that solemn silence came a storm of cries and curses, as their seamen went to work to fit the yard and raise the sail; while their fighting men seized their matchlocks and trained the guns. They were well commanded by an heroic able villian. Astern the consort thundered; but the Agra's response was a dead silence more awful than broadsides.

For then was seen with what majesty the enduring Anglo-Saxon fights.

One of the indomitable race on the gangway, one at the foremast, two at the wheel, conned and steered the great ship down on a hundred matchlocks, and a grinning broadside, just as they would have conned and steered her into a British harbor.

"Starboard!" said Dodd, in a deep calm voice, with a motion of his hand.

"Starboard it is."

The pirate wriggled ahead a little. The man forward made a silent signal to Dodd.

"Port!" said Dodd, quietly.

"Port it is."

But at this critical moment the pirate astern sent a mischievous shot, and knocked one of the men to atoms at the helm.

Dodd waved his hand without a word, and another man rose from the deck, and took his place in silence, and laid his unshaking hand on the wheel stained with that man's warm blood whose place he took.

The high ship was now scarce sixty yards distant: she seemed to know: she reared her lofty figurehead with great awful shoots into the air.

But now the panting pirates got their new foresail hoisted with a joyful shout: it drew, the schooner gathered way, and their furious consort close on the Agra's heels just then scourged her deck with grape.

"Port!" said Dodd, calmly.

"Port it is."

The giant prow darted at the escaping pirate. That acre of coming canvas took the wind out of the swift schooner's foresail; it flapped: oh, then she was doomed!... CRASH! the Indiaman's cut-water in thick smoke beat in the schooner's broadside: down went her masts to leeward like fishing-rods whipping the water; there was a horrible shrieking yell; wild forms leaped off on the Agra, and were hacked to pieces almost ere they reached the deck—a surge, a chasm in the ear, filled with an instant rush of engulfing waves, a long, awful, grating, grinding noise, never to be forgotten in this world, all along under the ship's keel—and the fearful majestic monster passed on over the blank she had made, with a pale crew standing silent and awestruck on her deck; a cluster of wild heads and staring eyeballs bobbing like corks in her foaming wake, sole relic of the blotted-out Destroyer; and a wounded man staggering on the gangway, with hands uplifted and staring eyes.

www.ingramcontent.com/pod-product-compliance
Lightning Source LLC
Chambersburg PA
CBHW020350130626
46549CB00003B/1387